First edition 2018
Library of Congress Control Number: 2017956677
ISBN 978-1-60991-209-3 (USA)
ISBN 978-178475-970-4 (UK)

10 9 8 7 6 5 4 3 2 1

Printed in China

This book was typeset in Athelas.
The illustrations were created traditionally
and in mixed media.
Book design by Rose Audette

Ripley Entertainment Inc.
7576 Kingspointe Parkway, Suite 188
Orlando, Florida 32819
Email: publishing@ripleys.com
visit us at www.ripleys.com/books

Young Arrow
20 Vauxhall Bridge Road
London SW1V 2SA

Young Arrow is part of the Penguin Random House
group of companies whose addresses can be found at
global.penguinrandomhouse.com.

 Penguin
Random House
UK

First published in Great Britain in 2018
by Young Arrow

www.penguin.co.uk

A CIP catalogue record for
this book is available from
the British Library.

BREMNER
and the Party

Carrie Bolin and Jessica Firpi

Illustrated by John Graziano

RIPLEY
PUBLISHING

a Jim Pattison Company

My name is Bremner.
I'm a puffer fish.

I'm going to a party.

Gulp. Tonight.

What if no one
else shows up?

I'm sure everyone will already be there.

I bet they all know
each other.

No one else will be nervous.

I hope I don't
puff up.

What if no one talks to me?

I really don't want to puff up.

Don't puff up. Don't puff up. Don't puff up.